Moo Moo Mooing

igloobooks

The cows in the meadow are **moo-moo-mooing**, chomping on the green grass, **chew-chew-chewing**.

Moo goes one cow and moo goes another.
Moo-moo-moo go all the cows together.

Moo-moo-chew on the noisy little farm.

Oink-oink-oink go the pigs in the sty,
snuffling in the mud as the tractor chugs by.

Here comes the swill with a **sploosh-sploosh-splosh.**

chomp-Slurp-chomp go the pigs in the trough.

Oink-splosh-Slurp on the noisy little farm.

The ducks in the pond are...

... quack-quack-quacking,

nestling in the nest where the eggs are **cracking**.

A crick... a crack... then, tiny little wings.
Peep-peep-peep go the new ducklings.

Moo!

Quack-crack-peep on the noisy little farm.

The gruff billy goats are **bleat-bleat-bleating...**

... **crunching** all the cabbages, **eat-eat-eating.**

The broody hens are scratch-scratch-scratching...

... clucking at the cute chicks hatch-hatch-hatching

He's got apples and carrots and nice fresh hay.
Clip-clop go the horses as they **neigh-neigh-neigh**.

Toot-hoot-neigh on the noisy little farm.

Vrmm-vrmm-Vrmm

goes Farmer Ben's truck.

In the meadow, the sheep are stuck.

The kittens in the kitchen are **lap-lap-lapping.**

The puppies in the basket are
yap-yap-yapping.

Woof-woof-**meow,** they chase and play.

It's very noisy in the farmhouse today.

Lap-yap-**meow** on the noisy little farm.

The golden sun is Sink-Sink-Sinking.

All the little stars are happily twinkling.

Moo!

Evening shadows
come slowly **creeping**.

Soon, all the animals will be **sleeping**.
Creep-creep-sleep on the noisy little farm.

The cows in the field stop **mooing** and **chewing**.

There's no more **clucking** or **munching** or **scratching**.
No more **quacking**, **cracking**, **oinking** or **bleating**.

No more splooshing, slurping, tooting, hooting, scratching, hatching, yapping or lapping.

Zzzz-zzzz-ZZZZ.

Everyone's asleep on the quiet little farm.